The Child's World

Published in the United States of America by The Child's World®
1980 Lookout Drive • Mankato, MN 56003-1705
800-599-READ • www.childsworld.com

ACKNOWLEDGMENTS
The Child's World®: Mary Berendes, Publishing Director
The Design Lab: Kathleen Petelinsek, Design and Page Production
Literacy Consultants: Cecilia Minden, PhD, and Joanne Meier, PhD

LIBRARY OF CONGRESS
CATALOGING-IN-PUBLICATION DATA
Moncure, Jane Belk.
  My "m" sound box / by Jane Belk Moncure ;
illustrated by Rebecca Thornburgh.
    p. cm. – (Sound box books)
  Summary: "Little m has an adventure with items beginning with
his letter's sound, such as mice, muddy monkeys, and a magic
moon machine."–Provided by publisher.
  ISBN 978-1-60253-153-6 (library bound : alk. paper)
  [1. Alphabet.] I. Thornburgh, Rebecca McKillip, ill. II. Title. III.
Series.
  PZ7.M739Mym 2009
  [E]–dc22   2008033169

A NOTE TO PARENTS AND EDUCATORS:

Magic moon machines and five fat frogs are just a few of the fun things you can share with children by reading books with them. Reading aloud helps children in so many ways! It introduces them to new words, motivates them to develop their own reading skills, and expands their attention span and listening abilities. So it's important to find time each day to share a book or two . . . or three!

As you read with young children, you can help develop their understanding of how print works by talking about the parts of the book—the cover, the title, the illustrations, and the words that tell the story. As you read, use your finger to point to each word, modeling a gentle sweep from left to right.

Simple word games help develop important prereading skills, including an understanding of rhyme and alliteration (when words share the same beginning sound, such as "six" and "sand"). Try playing with words from a book you've just shared: "What other words start with the same sound as moon?" "Cat and hat, do those words rhyme?" The possibilities are endless—and so are the rewards!

My "m" Sound Box®

WRITTEN BY JANE BELK MONCURE

ILLUSTRATED BY REBECCA THORNBURGH

Little  had a box. "I will find things that begin with my **m** sound," he said. "I will put them into my sound box."

Little  found monkeys. Did he put the monkeys into his box?

He did.

Then Little  found a mouse.

Then he found another mouse,

and another mouse.

He found many mice!

Did he put the mice into the box

with the monkeys? He did.

But the monkeys did not like the mice. The monkeys were mad!

They jumped out of the box and

ran up a mountain.

Little  ran up the mountain.

The mice ran up the mountain, too.

Then the monkeys ran down the mountain.

The monkeys were so mad, they did not see the mud!

The monkeys fell into the mud!

Now they were very mad.

What a mess!

Little  and the mice pulled

the monkeys out of the mud.

The monkeys were still mad.

Little 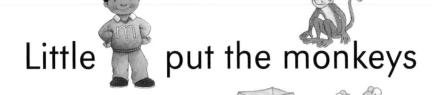 put the monkeys

back into the box. "Mice, be

nice!" he said.

"I must find something else for

my mice," said Little .

Just then, Little  met a moose. "Moose," he said,

"you are just what I need for my mice."

Little  saw a merry-go-round.

"Let's ride the merry-go-round,"

he said.

He found some money. They all

went for a ride on the

merry-go-round.

Then Little  looked up and saw the moon. "The moon belongs in my box!" he said.

"How can I get the moon?"

Just then, Little 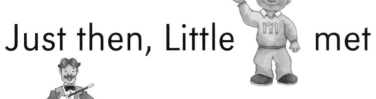 met
a magician.

"The moon is too big for your  box," said the magician.

"But I will take you to the moon in my magic moon machine."

And he did!

He took them all the way to the
moon. Some magic!

Little 's Word List

machine

magic

magician

merry-go-round

mice

money

monkey

moon

moose

mountain

mouse

mud

Other Words with Little

magnet

mailbox

map

marbles

marshmallow

mask

milk

mittens

mop

motorcycle

mouth

mug

mushroom

mustard

More to Do!

Little  found lots of things to put in his box. Let's make a silly rhyme about some of them! See if you can guess the rhyming words in this silly story.

A Rhyming Story:

1. One happy monkey walking along,
   Skipping and hopping and singing a _____.

2. Some mice came by and asked to play.
   "Let's have some fun! It's a beautiful _____!"

3. "Let's run up the mountain. That sounds like fun!
   It's a nice warm day because of the _____."

4. They all had fun until the sun went down.
   "It's time to go home," said the monkey with a _____.

5. "There's Mr. Moon. He'll show us our house.
   Thanks for the fun!" said one gray _____.

ANSWERS:
1. song   4. frown
2. day   5. mouse
3. sun

Now you try! See if you can make up some rhyming stories using these word groups:

cat/hat/pat/bat/mat

bee/three/tree/knee/free

dog/frog/log/fog/bog

clown/town/brown/gown/crown

About the Author

Best-selling author Jane Belk Moncure has written over 300 books throughout her teaching and writing career. After earning a Master's degree in Early Childhood Education from Columbia University, she became one of the pioneers in that field. In 1956, she helped form the Virginia Association for Early Childhood Education, which established the first statewide standards for teachers of young children.

Inspired by her work in the classroom, Mrs. Moncure's books have become standards in primary education, and her name is recognized across the country. Her success is reflected not only in her books' popularity with parents, children, and educators, but also by numerous awards, including the 1984 C. S. Lewis Gold Medal Award.

About the Illustrator

Rebecca Thornburgh lives in a pleasantly spooky old house in Philadelphia. If she's not at her drawing table, she's reading—or singing with her band, called Reckless Amateurs. Rebecca has one husband, two daughters, and two silly dogs.